GW00492721

About Leaf Books

Leaf Books' fine and upstanding mission is to support the publication of high quality short fiction, micro-fiction and poetry by both new and established writers.

We have put over 300 authors and poets into print since our inception in 2006. Many of them have never been published before.

See our website at www.leafbooks.co.uk for news, more information about our authors, other titles and having your own work published by Leaf.

Other Leaf Books Anthologies

Ada
and
more
Nano-Fiction

First published by Leaf Books Ltd in 2009

Copyright © The Authors
Cover Design © Sarah Emily Edmonds

www.leafbooks.co.uk

Leaf Books Ltd.
GTi Suite,
Valleys Innovation Centre,
Navigation Park,
Abercynon,
CF45 4SN

Printed by Jem
www.jem.co.uk

ISBN-10: 1-905599-50-1
ISBN-13: 978-1-905599-50-9

Contents

Introduction

We wanted tiny stories, 'cause that cliché about small packages isn't so foolish. So we opened a competition for stories of 100 words or fewer and received a delightfully crazy number of entries. Here's the result. Real tiny stories. Fulfilling narratives without the commitment. Read 'Ada', our brilliant winner, and all our brilliant runners-up, and wonder what novelists want with those 89,900 extra words.

Note that intros can be kept to 100 words or fewer as well.

The competition was judged by the Leaf Team.

Our thanks to all who entered.

The Stories

Ada

by Lyn Browne

I always told mother 'Don't you die on washday' and now she has, as if I didn't have enough to do, the water to be carried in and my hands cracking. The Lord is my Shepherd. Now there's blood on her collar where I stroked her neck. Lovely skin she had, it only wrinkled in the last few weeks. Be strong in the grace that is Christ Jesus.

I must keep the boys away. I'm holding on to mother and they're whooping out in the lane and there'll be another pile of washing soon. This lovely white blouse, I pressed it for her last week. Whites are always the worst, especially when they were babies, all those petticoats. Dolly-blue to make the whites whiter and now she's gone and died.

February 15th 2003

by Wayne Foster

A man with a beard seized the opportunity to rest his end of the banner and open a thermos. The small bloc behind him – a university classics department or an amateur dramatics group – slowed up against his back, sharing a joke. This parenthesis rippled backwards so that looking towards Trafalgar Square you could see banner after banner slowing to a stop. You could imagine this break dominoing back to Embankment, so that long after the bearded man had closed his flask and continued, the march would stop, and this would be why.

Arrival

by Sue Anderson

It was such a strange world, full of glaring lights and harsh sounds. She cried when she saw it, screamed and kicked, waving her clumsy limbs, fighting to get back where she had come from.

Eventually she gave up and nestled into the softness beside her. It smelt good, and presently she found a place to put her mouth. She drank in warmth and comfort. Memories of the time before were fainter now, but the link wasn't completely broken. The longing persisted: that would never quite go.
She just had to find another way to get there.

The Death of Magic

by Sarah Armstrong

She bent to stroke the yellow petals. 'This flower can make you happy forever.'

He frowned. 'How?'

'You just eat it. It's magic,' she smiled. 'And secret.'

'How do *you* know, then?'

She shrugged. 'That's secret too.'

'But it might be poisonous. Have you tried it?'

'Don't you trust me?'

He hesitated. 'Yes, normally, but ….'

'Okay, don't try it.' She straightened. 'Don't be happy.'

'But I do want to be happy.'

'So trust me.'

He picked it and looked at her. 'Are you sure?'

'You're making me doubt it now.' Hot tears made her eyes ache. 'What have you done?'

The Last Supper

by Holly Atkinson

It's the only tin left. The cupboards are bare. All the boxes are stacked; all the cutlery bar one knife, fork and spoon, packed away. In the jostling dark at the back of the cupboard its label has come away, so dinner will be a surprise. Some airless mystery food, suspended in time. I practice the words I'll need to know – forchette, couteau, cuiller – as I peel off the lid. They roll around my tongue, as fat and unwelcome as the prunes in my mouth. The juice dribbles from my chin and splashes on the map I cannot read.

Written on the wall

by Holly Atkinson

It looks just like a bare wall. But there, see, the hook where the smiling photograph hung. Down there, the stain where the red wine splashed from her hand as they danced. Over here, the grubby fingerprints of toddlers growing higher and higher.

He made that dent there by smashing his fist into the wall. The mirror left that dirty rectangle, where she would glance and not recognise the woman she had become, the deep dark circles beneath her eyes. And all along there, see, the scuff marks the careless furniture removal men made, after the cracks began to show.

Discovery

by Christine Axon

Strolling through a crisp autumn forest, my dog unearths the body of a small child. My blood runs as cold as the air and I look down in fear and disbelief.

A tree creaks. I turn in haste, expecting a crazed axe man or a lamenting mother blaming me for her loss. But it's just the wind playing with nature. I look back and he hasn't moved.

I turn to run, calling the dog, but he doesn't follow. Branches whipping at my face, I have to find somebody to tell.

I imagine the boy running with other children above me.

Things to Do Before Breakfast

by Chloe Banks

If I hadn't gone outside to discover why the kid by my gate was crying I wouldn't have known he'd missed the school bus. Then I wouldn't have given him a lift and he would have got behind in his work and probably fallen in with the wrong crowd and ended up leading a life of crime. Maybe he would have become a gangster who corrupted the government, leading to civil and then world war. We'd all have been annihilated in a million nuclear blasts.

So yeah, I *was* late for work; but I did save the world before breakfast.

The Dentist

by K.M. Bainbridge

Mr Harrison had suede shoes and suede hair. His yellow socks shouted, 'Untrustworthy!' even to the child I was. His practice in Bellevue Terrace was next door to Maynard's and opposite the biscuit factory and, the one time I remember visiting him, he gassed me and had his way with my small mouth.

Like a conjurer he had a glamorous assistant. When I surfaced in the recovery room, his wife, coiffed, lipsticked and red-taloned, was leaning into me like a ravenous bird. I screamed and blood oozed down my chin.

Life's mysteries deepened for me that day.

Puff

by Adam Bealby

I started smoking when I was a nipper. It was just something us young dragons did to impress the supposedly virginal maidens. I used to have this trick where I'd light everyone up with an arc of nostril-flame. Now I'm lucky if I can muster a spark. The cancer's in my wing-stumps. I can't fly anymore, never mind frolic in the autumn mist. What good's a cave full of gold if you aren't around to spend it? I'd say to anyone still smoking: give up now before it's too late. You don't want to end up a mythical creature.

Lucky Escape

by Angus Binnie

During work on a harbour, a digger operator escaped death when his machine fell into a hole. Fortunately, the man jumped clear before his expensive digger disappeared for good. The depth of the hole is horrendous.

Incoming tide drained away into the hole and a bystander said it was like bath water running out. Filling the hole with rubble will be tried.

The digger driver, a keen golfer, said, 'It's the nearest I'll get to a hole in one.'

A Marine Geologist reported, 'If they cannot plug this soon we will lose much of the North Sea.'

A Simple Mistake

by Jackie Blake

It was a mistake. A simple mistake. Everyone makes them. How could he throw her out like that? Why couldn't he see that she loved him? Worshipped him, in fact. Didn't everyone deserve a second chance? After all, she'd only chewed one of his best shoes. The other one was fine.

Everything You Hate You Will Become

by John Blunden

Steve held a gun to the head of Surrealism, threatening to blow its brains out for what it had done to comedy in recent years.

'Say your prayers,' Steve said calmly. 'You have no place here in comedy or any offshoots of its form.'

'Look,' Surrealism said, 'even the fact that you're talking to me suggests your surrealist nature. Does that not make you a hypocrite?'

Realising this was true, he turned the gun onto Irony instead.

Nice Things

by John Blunden

Ug looked out of her cave over to Grug's, which was well lit and warm. Ug's husband, Urg, drew on the walls.

'Ug want fire,' said Ug to her husband. 'Grug have fire in cave Grug. Why we not have fire?'

'Ug want moon on stick,' grunted Urg, not looking away from his cave drawings. 'Fire passing fashion statement. Grug idiot. Nobody want fire in a few years: trust Urg.'

Ug sighed. She never got anything nice.

County Court

by Tom Bowen and Noggin

The Aberystwyth County Court judge's chambers used to be part of the converted ballroom of a former hotel. The newly appointed judge, black-robed with purple sash and cuffs and fresh white wig, revolved slowly between two floor-to-ceiling mirrors fixed on opposite walls, as he admired his reflected figure diminishing to infinity in both directions. With his arms raised he moved his head from side to side to get a better view. When he noticed a bus queue outside watching him, enraptured, he stopped pirouetting and bowed low. They clapped, waved and filed onto the bus, which drove away, tooting.

Best Friend

by Tom Bowen and Noggin

Oh no! Here he is again, lowering himself gingerly onto the stairs so that he comes nose to nose, literally within a whisker of me where I lie in my favourite position, tucked tight against the riser of the next step.

He stares at me from rheumy eyes behind smeared bifocals. Talk about windows of the soul! What about letting sleeping dogs lie? And to think that people use the expression dog's breath as a term of abuse.

Fortunately, when I wag my tail, he'll get up and leave me in peace. It's called a Pavlovian reaction.

Dystokia

by Sarah Boyd

Colin clutched his tea, inhaling its sweetness to cover the farm smell to which he had become unaccustomed. The clock ticked on uninterrupted for twelve minutes. Colin entertained himself by placing his elbows on the table and watching his father's disapproval. The only other distraction was the old man's rattling breaths.

Eventually, Colin remarked, 'Could look at my room now, if you're ready.'

'Not *your* room anymore, boy.'

Colin sighed, resisting the urge to rush upstairs and slam his door. His father was right, the room wasn't his anymore, but there was no need to say it like that.

Reading Dostoyevsky and Thinking About Crisps

by Sarah Boyd

The train chugga-chuggas away and Nina presses against the seatback, tights rasping softly as she crosses her legs. She draws from an internal pocket a thick book, its spine creased and cracked, and bends her head to it. Every few minutes, she flips a page and, although her eyes don't move across the text, she appears absorbed. Occasionally, her glance flicks upwards, falling casually but consistently upon a bespectacled man across the aisle. Each time he fails to look over, she gently adjusts the book's angle, so the words *The Brothers Karamazov* are visible to anyone looking that way.

Fishing Tackle

by Ruth Brandt

My boyfriend went away to university, leaving his fishing tackle in my safe keeping. I took to hanging around the lake where he had fished, chatting to the other fishermen and telling them how much I missed him. When one of them caught a 26.6lb pike, I knew my boyfriend would be delighted to learn that the lake held a fish of such a size. So I took a photo of the pair, entitling it 'What a catch!' before texting it to him. My boyfriend texted back saying I should return his tackle to his mum.

Ducks

by Ruth Brandt

My boyfriend insisted that ducks couldn't fly. We argued for days, staying up late into the night. When I ran out of facts, I decided to give my boyfriend the time and space to process all my compelling arguments.

After a week of silence I returned to our flat to find that my boyfriend remained convinced that ducks were purely water birds. In order to put the silly argument behind us and get on with our lives, I persuaded him to accompany me to the park. We waited by the duck pond for an hour. The ducks didn't fly.

Invincible

by Rosie Brown

Her eyes sparkle, like they did that night under the Town Hall chandeliers. She was young in her dress of peach flushed satin, as he whirled her round, vital, in a world where anything could happen.

Later, they brought me into a world they weren't so sure of, and some dreams slipped away. We look at his photograph and he's still smiling.

Memories wither, but this one is as fresh as the flowers on their Golden Wedding day.

An echo reels in my head. Music that no air raid siren can deafen.

Runners in the Sun

by Linda Cairns

Apart from a distant clatter of a train, the only sound is the breeze in the trees and my running footsteps. I've left behind the muted light and pleasant musty smell of the woodland track and, as I leap down from the stile into the open field, I'm startled by intense light as if emerging from a cinema in mid-afternoon. Out in the sun, I see a tall, lean runner keeping in pace with me. She's wearing exactly the same clothes but I'm envious of how tall and lean she looks stretched out on the ground ahead.

May Queen

by Jan Cascarini

'Persuade her!' commanded the mother.

'Impossible,' said the father.

'She's ungovernable,' whispered the courtiers.

The first suitor knelt to plead his cause.

'Perhaps …' the princess answered.

The second suitor begged with tears in his eyes.

'Possibly …' said the princess, turning away.

The third suitor flashed a dazzling smile and strode around displaying his spectacular musculature, expecting a result.

'I'll think about it,' was the disdainful reply.

'Eric,' she said to the gardener's boy, 'give me one of those luscious peaches.'

'In your dreams,' he laughed, wheeling his barrow away down the path.

And he was, that very night.

'I did see you. I glimpsed you for a second.'

by Apala Chowdhury

All I could think was thank God I ran out of petrol last night and had to leave the car there; thank God I didn't run in wearing my grotty running gear when I couldn't find my trainers; thank God I got off the bus several stops early 'cause of my hangover; thank God I took Upper Street and not Liverpool Road when I nearly turned left; thank God I didn't buy that coffee; thank God I was wearing my favourite outfit, walking past you – *and her* – on my best side … and you saw me for a blinking, bloody second?

The Bought Complexion

by Mary Cookson

Driving home on Valentine's Day I stop to buy him chocolates. I know that I promised undying love but it's difficult with my job to be constant and true to life. I'm a peddler of marvels. As a traveller in beauty products I unearth those women who buy their complexions privately and guide them back into the world.

With the sudden news of his passing I know that my lover's complexion will lack lustre.

The mortician appears shocked at my normal request.

'He let me make him up in life,' I say. 'Why not in death?'

Revival

by Anne Cooper

'Had a heart attack, yes,' Rose told her daughter gently. 'She's in Kings.'

'Okay.'

'I'd go soon if I were you. She might seem ... might not be quite herself.'

When Layla arrived Gran was sitting up in bed, smiling. 'Isn't it wonderful!' Light flooded the ward. Layla pulled up a chair.

'They treating you all right?'

'Oh yes. I like to imagine these nurses are prostitutes from the washhouses in Paris ... bathing, combing their hair.' Layla's eyes widened. 'You know, the painter Degas. He couldn't afford models.'

Layla sighed relief. 'Of course.'

'Wonder if they'd let me have my brushes in here.'

Jigsaw

by Una Corbett

The dog was long in the body. It looked as though an extra piece of the jigsaw had been put into its middle. She couldn't help thinking there must be another dog, missing a piece. Looking very short. In the body.

But you couldn't really afford to worry about it. Life's too short. She often told people.

Why was this dog so long? 'It's a beagle. It's supposed to look like that,' someone said. She must have asked out loud!

Still, she'd better start looking for the dog. Looking for the dog with the missing piece. Quickly. Before the bedtime bell.

Prelude

by Una Corbett

The young seamstress sits three places from the left. She sits in the third row back from the raised platform. The platform that reflects the audience as a glimpse of the season to come.

The season to come being summer, the theme is gauze and cotton and lace and floating satin ribbons. And hats that tip and turn to draw an imaginary line from outer eye towards the curve of a lip.

The music is Strauss and enchanting, and the audience smiles and sways and loves the feel of the summer to come.

The young seamstress notices the poster in flashes that startle. She feels attacked by the finger pointing at her. She wonders whether she, too, is needed by the fierce-looking man. She'll go along tomorrow to find out.

Invisible Love

by Dan Coxon

It wasn't easy being married to the Invisible Girl.

You'd think that spending your life with a superhero would be bliss, but it's tough washing bloodstains out of invisible clothes. It's even tougher lying next to someone whose presence amounts to nothing more than a few creases in the sheets. True, we only ever had to buy single tickets for the cinema, but often when I went to hold her hand I'd be left grasping at air.

When she finally left me I didn't notice for a week. Superheroes, it seems, don't need significant others.

Bandiera Rosa

by Shelley Day Sclater

Nobody knew what I was doing. Nobody even suspected. They thought I was throwing food out for the birds, silly old thing. Then they complained that the rats would get it, that they'd proliferate, foolish old hag. But come June there was a whole field of flowers like no-one ever saw. The old donkey stood bemused, knee deep in them. Tourists came from far and wide and went away with photographs. There is one of me in my red bandana, smiling in the wind, on the cover of Time.

Unwrapped

by Bobbie Darbyshire

Christmas lunch, secret Santa: four draw from the bag. Janet is thrilled with the brooch (which she wrapped this morning herself), Lil with the lavender scent (ditto), and Marian with her chic scarf. Discovering his gift, young Will blushes and laughs. Tonight, he will try on this red silk G-string again, and imagine Marian wearing her scarf. And her boots.

Revolution

by Morgan Downie

These are a people who will not use revolving doors. They believe in the power of transformation. One person goes in, another comes out, seamlessly, exchanging one body, one mind for another without the slightest realisation. They call this dynamic reincarnation. These are a people who will not use revolving doors until, overcome by despair or in that last moment before death, they throw themselves forward and, spinning, emerge as someone else.

David

by Nicholas Edwards

David was his name. This was his one word. Together they were a new type of family. The conditioning taught him that last names were a hazard to be avoided. But this one word wasn't enough for him anymore.

David's fingernail had scored grooves down pages of phonebooks in countless hotels. Any word familiar torn and hidden.

More words were locked inside David. A whole description of a person. How could five letters, just five, lead onto that?

David sits in the van reading place names from a map. David waits for answers. Repeats this one word so he won't forget.

Hairy and Scary

by Anne Elder

We had an aunt and uncle we called 'hairy' and 'scary' for obvious reasons. They kissed us goodnight with alcohol breath and roaming hands. Their grins loomed out of the darkness to meet our frightened eyes. I took up self-defence classes and karate-chopped their indiscretions right down the stairs. Mother was shocked and scolding but it didn't matter. Our evenings were ours again. We were free to create our own monsters without having them forced upon us, breathing down our necks, undermining our creativity, robbing us of our illusions.

Neighbours

by Gavin Eyers

Three months have passed.

Plums from Tom next door's tree lay splattered on my patio. I was going to sweep them away but decided they might make a special meal for some little visitor of the garden. I'm sitting on my wooden chair amongst the little purple explosions as if part of some hideous piece of modern art.

I'm stretching my neck and looking over the fence. He isn't there. He's avoided me since, you see, because he knows that I saw and that I know.

Sandwiches

by Amelia Fortnam

'How did it all begin? Now that's a question!' Mrs Talby wasn't, she had to be honest with herself, sensing the enrapture appropriate to her subject matter. 'Isn't it.' Rows of faces stayed furiously interested in their i-phones. She changed tack. 'Who believes that God created the world? Hmm?' A few hands up. That's the ticket: spark their interest with something contentious, then Bam! You'd have a theological discussion going. 'Who believes in evolution?' The same hands. She thought for a second. 'Who ate a crocodile this morning?' Again the same hands. 'For God's sake go and eat your sandwiches.'

The Secret Life of Life

by Dorothy Fryd

Life has a secret. It's about where things end up. Things that have been missed end up in the Seventeenth Century Sea. Things that should've been said by idle parents, strung-out lovers, repressed teenagers and Carmelite nuns end up in the Seventeenth Century Sea. What else goes in there is between everywhere and nowhere: the dead children who fell between incompetent and exceptional, excessive punctuation and unchartered thoughts. For example: what the cow thinks about the rain, how the horse silently bays about his ankylosing spondylitis and the desperate quandaries of an ant-intolerant Aardvark in the Savannah.

The Traveller

by Clare Girvan

After many days lost in the woods, a starving traveller cried out in desperation, 'Oh, Lord, if You exist, send me some food!'

A great storm arose, which sent a tree crashing to the ground, killing a wild pig and startling a bird into laying an egg that broke on a rock below. Lightning set fire to the tree, which began to roast the pig. Fat from the pig fried the egg on the heated rock, spattering onto some nearby wild mushrooms.

'Oh, Lord, I believe!' cried the traveller. 'I don't suppose you could manage a bit of fried bread?'

Rain

by Dee Gordon

I only went into the art gallery to escape the downpour. And there he was. The one.

Until then, I'd never believed in love at first sight. It was ridiculous. I knew nothing about him. He wasn't even good-looking. He was obviously artistic, studying the canvases closely, slowly, with interest.

Dare I approach him? I wasn't shy – just afraid that someone that intellectual would regard me with indifference, even distaste.

He must have felt my gaze, because he turned round. 'I hope you're not going to ask me anything about art.' He smiled. 'I'm only sheltering from the rain.'

The Addiction

by Ellie Hartland

For three years I existed.

    Wake up. Get money. Get drugs.

    Go to sleep.

    Wake up. Get money. Get drugs.

    Screwing for cash. Exist, not live.

    Then a missed period. Panic.

    An opiate addicted baby is born every 2 ½ minutes in the UK.

    Panic. Come clean to mum.

    Rehab for three months.

    Come clean then become clean.

    Baby bump growing.

    Need drugs. No, I say. No drugs.

Think of her.
Baby. Baby. Baby.
Hospital lights. Pain. Screaming.
White light tunnel pain like a crack hit striking the brain.
Pain.
Crying.
My baby crying.
My baby.
My beautiful new addiction.

Pick Ugly

by Sarah Hilary

Ayana's mother said, 'Pick ugly,' meaning fruit like pawpaw, tangerine. Picking ugly meant appreciating everything, giving thanks.

Ayana always chose the orange with the scarred skin. Juice filled her mouth with colour, ran down her chin.

She picked her husband the same way. Thomas was a good man, just a whole heap of ugly.

Thomas loved to watch Ayana putting fruit in wooden bowls, oranges grown in their garden during the summer when their bare feet brought dust into the little house.

The oranges ripened round, dimpled skins as bright as the taste they brought to Ayana's lips and his.

Disappointment

by Michelle Holhorea

I watched as she sauntered through the crowd along the platform. Ten years since we shared our last kiss, said our goodbyes. And there she was now, coming back. Back home. To me. The closer she got the bigger the jolt in my stomach. She hadn't changed much. Same cascade of honey hair falling over her shoulders. Beautiful brown eyes still wearing the same warm smile. There was only one thing missing there. The sign of recognition as she brushed past me.

She left a message on my phone later on. 'You didn't turn up'.

On Men and Cheeseboards

by Linda Houlton

Last night she'd had a Wensleydale with cranberries. He was an architect with the soul of an artist; he dressed buildings in scarlet ribbons and gauze but undressed her indifferently.

She thought him a pretentious wanker. He made her long for that rustic Double Gloucester, consumed with sweet fervour and dry cider on rolling Cotswold Hills.

And yes, she'd had her share of limp roulades but still cherished one idyllic dream. A dream so nearly fulfilled, until it was exposed as an impostor camembert.

So she prayed, 'Dear God, please send maturity and melting passion. Next time, deliver unto me a brie.'

Stepping Over

by Lauren Huxley-Blythe

Stealing the shoes was easy. Mairead sneaked into her sister's bedroom early on Tuesday morning. She tiptoed away, hugging them to smother her traitorous heart.

When she fastened the glossy straps around her ankles, the leather locked onto her skin. She loved the sensuous curve of her arched feet, her calves tightening and lifting above the spiky heels. She fizzed, transformed.

A strange compulsion steered her, tottering, traipsing down the stairs.

She tugged her flimsy nightie to prevent it ruching, ever-higher, up the goose-pimpled flesh of her exposed legs, powerless to halt the onward trajectory of their new direction.

Flight

by Flavia Idriceanu

The delight of a secret life at seventy! Nothing outrageous, really, only the thrill of detaching myself from the ground and floating feather-like. Only at home, especially for the stairs, which are painful to climb in the old way.

I discovered I could fly while watering my petunias. I thought 'Fred!', but he's dead and I'm no batty old woman confusing reality with entanglements of her mind. It's my secret: the children might worry about me falling down. Imagining perpetually-busy Anne chiding me for lounge levitating makes me giggle!

I'll say I broke my hip tripping over the rug.

We are the twenty-somethings of the post-apocalypse
by Grace Knight

We are the twenty-somethings of the post-apocalypse. We will raise our children on bicycle generators and old copies of *Vogue*. We will teach them to read from books on building maintenance while the old city falls around us. They will be carpenter-scholars, plumber-academics. They will chronicle our times in breathtaking verse and heartbreaking prose. We will build back. We will build better.

Except that there can be no children. Not from anyone. Not ever.

We are the twenty-somethings of the post-apocalypse and if we can't do it, no-one can.

Driving Away

by Kathy Kachelries

Driving away rather than towards through the cleft of the Grand Canyon, there is a hungry silence with no reception where cellphone power is nothing but battery drain. Signs indicate miles to the next stop but at three am the next stop is dark, pumps blank and so silent that even the stars hurt your ears. With the roof latch broken the wind is a lake, like swimming in April without a shore to lean against. Shivering and without horizon, you know that even if your tank ran empty, not even a trucker would stop.

The Old Bomb Shelter

by R.J. Marer

The old bomb shelter housed father's art studio. It was cockroach-infested; our community mocked him. But it offered protection from infernal heat with enough light for painting.

Together we'd spend afternoons being artists. Rainbow, a cultured 'roach, assisted in colour selection: he'd scramble over acrylics and oils then stop at his recommendation.

The day that war was declared again, sirens ululated; people cried for want of shelter. Huddled amidst Magenta, Indian Yellow and Viridian, they forgot about the war for a short while. The 'roaches stood guard at the entrance, keeping us safe.

Lost Plot

by Pauline Masurel

Have you seen my little black and white plot? Smudge on third page and large chunk missing from the end of its tale. Dearly-loved family saga, greatly missed. Last seen in early stages of character development. Tends to wander. Please check your shed in case my story's stowed away inside.

Jealousies

by Emily Midorikawa

Although he stopped me from meeting her ever again, my husband eventually forgave me. Just as I'm sure her husband would have forgiven her too, had she not moved to a flat three streets away and started going out all the time. Poor man, he must see her most evenings as I do walking off into town, her handbag swinging.

Losing It

by Beverley Mulliner

I pick up the gloves and place them on a windowsill. Further on, a scarf lies discarded on a chair. On the stairs is a jacket, followed by a sweater. My pace quickens. Trainers and socks are scattered before a closed door. I enter and see a t-shirt drooping from a coat-hook.

I press on, adding pair of faded jeans to the bundle of clothes I'm carrying.

The underwear is on the floor by the couch. The woman, naked, is curled foetus-like on its padded top.

'I've found your clothes,' I tell her.

'It's my mind I've lost,' she says.

Final Call

by Lyn O'Kelly

It's 7pm and loyal patrons are waiting. Marge has hollered the five-minute warning and Scarlet is still powdering the same cheek. Every time the tone is perfect, sweat and tears ruin the rosy circles in revolting patterns down her face. Insane, she mumbles lines to herself that are neither hers nor in the right order. The room was only reassuringly chaotic for a short time. Now everyone else is in their positions. Roger is on the curtains. Elsie is at the grand piano. Scarlet is still powdering. Her brother wouldn't pay the ticket fare tonight. Her father is dead.

David Dimbleby

by Phil O'Shea

I have only met a celebrity once in my life. It was David Dimbleby, the political commentator. He was a lot smaller than he looks on the telly. He was only about an inch high. I didn't really notice how small he was at first, but it slowly became apparent. The biggest clue to his miniature stature happened just after I had hole-punched some documents. I was emptying out the white paper circles from the hole-punch, and one of them fell towards the tiny political pundit, and just before it landed on him, he screamed, 'Oh no, it's the moon!'.

Replacement Teacher

by Gavin Parish

She had been a good teacher, one of the best – we absolutely *had* to clone her when the original wore out. Our policy of retaining staff DNA ensures continuity and the highest teaching standards. The transition is usually seamless, without pupils, colleagues or immediate family noticing a thing.

In Mrs McKenna's case, we made one vital error. On the day her DNA was extracted, she had been bitten by the class hamster. Her popularity with the kids was now at an all-time high, from the moment she started shredding textbooks for her nest in the corner of the classroom.

Think Tank

by Jonathan Pinnock

… Water … water … water … bingo! That's it! Sorted! A cure for aids, cancer and Alzheimer's! And, wow, I can see how to sort out the banking crisis, stop global warming and get cheap, clean energy for ever! Oh, and I know how we can have peace in the Middle East too! Woo-hoo! And I've got a workable unified field theory, and maybe a proof of the Riemann hypothesis! I just need to tell everyone somehow … maybe if I flap my fins so they catch the light and … water … water … water ….

Man Answers Door

by Pamela Pottinger

To reach the front door, Arthur has first to climb up several steps. After this he must negotiate, warily, a dimly lit narrow passage that gives out into a hallway equally devoid of light. It is a slow job. He has to catch his breath halfway. When the doorbell rings again it is sharp against his nerves.

At last he opens the door, and the brightness of the day dazzles him, sunlight squeezing his eyes tight, causing tears to rise.

And the caller?

Is long gone.

Statues

by John Ravenscroft

Saturday morning, two white bandaged figures appeared in the shopping mall. A sign asked if they were human or automatons.

Fred walked by with his motorised sweeper, eyeing those two statues as they occasionally moved an arm or head.

'One way to find out,' he thought.

He drove at them. They stood motionless until the brushes touched their feet.

To this day Fred doesn't know which one threw him into the fountain. He gave descriptions to the police, but his assailants were never seen again.

Two gorillas now occupy the space. Their eyes follow him. Fred stays well away.

A Night In

by Clare Reddaway

The slot swallows the borrowed DVD. I press play. The picture is not *Lark Rise*, as anticipated. The video is amateur but clear. A head swathed in a chequered keffiyeh; a chin, newly bearded. I listen to threats, unspecified; promises, grandiose; suicide, guaranteed. I watch, my hand still on my mobile, sweat prickling my skull. I know the Anglo Saxon face, can whisper with the home counties voice. I press his number, am unsurprised to shunt straight to voicemail. I dither between police and friends. Eventually, I sit immobilised and wait for the catastrophe of my brother and his bomb.

The Dead Old Lady's Tights

by Jemma Regan

They lay there to rest. Not a final resting place, but a new one – the stocking drawer at the Salvation Army charity shop. The lady died. An anonymous stranger. She never got to wear them.

I am looking for a Halloween costume.

Excited at the range of thrift store possibilities, I rummage through boxes and rifle through hangers. I feel a snag of sadness that tears into a ladder of eerie sentimentality. The packet of white tights, unopened. They would be perfect to draw black spiders and cobwebs on. A witch's treat.

I buy, customise, wear and discard them.

They Said it Wouldn't Last
by Martin Richards

She parked outside the house, took the rifle from its case and levelled it at the bedroom. I didn't know this was happening at the time or I would probably have moved from the window sooner.

She wept at my hospital bed, exclaiming unyielding love but never making eye contact. My eyes were all I could move then so my statement took over a week to write.

Nowadays, they have wheelchair ramps for visitors to the prison and, although our marriage hasn't had the perfect start, our friends all agree we seem to be getting on a lot better now.

Better
by Andy Rigley

'I think we're better together than anyone else in the world,' Laura says into my ear, her breath all vodka, coke and cigarettes.

I reply, staring at the cracks in the peach-lit ceiling, 'You think?'

She shifts her pale body up onto one elbow and runs her finger down the centre of my wet chest. 'Of course,' she laughs into my face, her stark red hair tickling my cold nose. 'Otherwise, what's the point?'

And at that very moment I finally found God. And God would forgive me in the morning.

Greg The Adventurer

by Gary Robins

The tourists love Greg. In the pub he amazes them with knowledge of their home-towns and countries; they give him maps and guidebooks in return. His few 'friends' do the same when returning from holidays. But they find him boring. He never shuts up. He lives with his mother. The walls and ceiling of his room are plastered with maps and he lies in bed staring at them: travelling the world in his dreams, sailing distant seas, racing over wild, wondrous landscapes and visiting far off exotic cities. Tourists love Greg the adventurer. Who has never left the village.

Henry's Breakfast is Still Here

by Nancy Saunders

My brother Henry's been missing for twenty-three hours, gone since yesterday's breakfast. He is two years younger than me, and I'm seven. Nobody's moved his bowl off the table, all his coco-pops have disappeared and the milk is brown and murky. Mam was shouting at Dadda, Dadda threw his cup of tea at the wall and it's still there now like a big splatt, like the wall is bleeding. I put my toast in my pocket and ran out the door. Should of taken Henry with me. He was sitting still as an icicle, his face white as a ghost.

We Love You, *Antiques Roadshow*

by Nancy Saunders

Dad took us to sea in a bargain car-boot dinghy. Found the beach, no bother. With Dad's map-reading there wasn't a hope of getting lost.

'Here we are then. Rhossili!' Dad's words barked from him like a polished sign.

There was a heavy suggestion of clouds. The beach was deserted. Normal people had warmer things to be doing with their January Sundays.

The boat looked like something you'd play with in the bath.

We clung on like limpets. Dad sliced through the waves. The coldness soaked through to our bones. All hope anchored on the *Antiques Roadshow*. Dad never missed.

Changing Days Two

by Jackie Sullivan

I'm running, loving the breeze, clutching my chest. Linda shouts wait and I'm glad to. We link arms, treading whitened sandals through melted tarmac.

I tell Mum, *they hurt when I run*! Ask your sister, she says, turning back to the stove, she'll find you something.

I feel mortified, but not at Mum. The dress she ran up from a remnant goes up at the back, showing the bare backs of her knees. I love her ferociously, no less so next day when I turn up at Kingstone Primary in Aunt Edie's whale-bone bra that comes down to my waist.

A Bad Hair Day

by Jayne Thickett

He's here again; I can hear him. Like the caterwauling of a randy tom. I go to the window and throw down my hair, bracing myself against the frame. He's no Slim-Jim. I think he'll pull my scalp off one of these days. Well, I've had my fun, so I tell him.

'Listen, Charming. Isn't it about time you brought a rope?'

'A rope?' he wheezes, uncomprehending.

'Yeah. So I can get out of here too.'

'Oh! Right. How come I never thought of that?'

'I wonder.' And I roll my eyes. Men.

Lungs

by Andrew Thorn

I sit in my zen garden. Death is there too.

'Hi, Joe,' I say. We're on first name terms, death and I.

Death looks down. 'I messed up the lines in your sand,' he says.

'The oxygen delivery guy does more damage than you.'

He leans in towards me, close to my face. 'Coming?'

I shake my head.

He grins. 'Gotta come one day.'

I take a long drag on my cigarette, and blow smoke in his face. 'Yup, but not today,' I grin back.

Death stomps off, kicking the sand about. 'Medical science,' he mutters.

Pianissimo

by Sandy Tippett

The van, neatly parked, tailgate down, was primed to receive its precious cargo. Annabelle, trimly tidy, felt nervous and guilty about giving her piano away, but happy it had found a good home. She checked her mobile. Weren't the people John had promised to send a bit late? She glanced up. Striding down the street towards her were five men: all different heights, all grinning broadly, all dressed in black, tattooed and wearing Doc Martins. Pierced all over and all sporting brightly coloured Mohican haircuts. Accompanied by one shaggy dog. She grinned back. Five punks to move the piano. Perfect.

Mirth

by Robin Tompkins

This is an incident that happened in the coffee bar of a department store, before the smoking ban. I have never understood it; perhaps you will.

This big old black guy lopes in, crumpled polyester suit, scowling through a three-day stubble.

He sits, props up a faded photo of a woman in the ashtray and glares at it.

Carefully, he sets fire to one corner with a cheap lighter. Then he begins to laugh. He laughs so hard his eyes water and he has to take off his thick spectacles to wipe them.

Until then, I liked laughter.

Déjà vu

by Steve Tymms

He sat there as, for the twelfth time that day, his Mum repeated, 'I do puzzles to keep my brain active. My mother had dementia, and it was horrible'.

He wanted to shout, 'I know. You already told me,' but he just smiled and said, 'Good plan, Mum'.

It was getting harder to take. And his kids seemed to be coping with this better than him.

That was thirty years ago.

Now he sits there telling his son, 'I do puzzles every day to keep my brain active. My mother had dementia, and it was horrible'.

His son just smiles.

First Date

by Wendy Vaughan

Amy grasped the black case of the new pink lipstick in her fist. It was hard to outline your mouth when your whole body shook but finally she had a pink slash across her face. Not too bad for a first attempt.

Time to face the class.

And him.

She pulled her sticky lips into what she hoped was a smile. He nodded at her. They manoeuvred their wheelchairs together as close as they could without being told to sit at other sides of the classroom.

Amy could read the message on his communication board.

Beautiful it said.

The Haulier

by Pete Walsh

My mother was in love with the doctor – I'm sure of it. I think she had children just so she could see the doctor.

The doctor put his hands inside my mother, hauling me and seven siblings from her womb. What he did changed my life.

Whenever I saw him, he'd use a sympathetic voice, look with sympathetic eyes and touch with strong sympathetic hands.

My younger brother looks like the doctor, taller than us, with dark hair and eyes, his mouth.

When taken for jabs, I could see, could sense, my mother was in love with the doctor.

Ghost Story

by Guy Ware

He knew there were no ghosts.

Yet once, when she was not there – when she was out, no more – he heard her voice. It called his name, once: calm, secure, unequivocally her.

And, when the raised hairs settled, he knew how it would be, when she had gone.

Rat Boy

by Robert Warrington

Rat Boy had rats in his back room. At first, being an unusual person, he didn't really mind. He gave them old-fashioned English names such as Betty and Mabel and Nigel and so forth.

Then the rats started eating him out of house and home. Reluctantly he phoned the exterminator, Derek. Surprisingly, Derek turned out to be a six-foot rodent.

All the rats began to worship Derek, thinking he was the rat god. Derek let this go on for a while. He seemed to enjoy it.

Then he put them down humanely and for a very reasonable price.

Straight Talking

by Sue Wilsea

I left my hair straighteners on today and burnt the house down. Not completely but we'll have to move out for several months. Mum went hysterical and had to be sedated while Dad's face went a weird grey colour like a zombie.

I was sorry (DUH! Obviously) but it wasn't like I meant to do it.

'We should have had a smoke alarm,' I said to Dad. PC Tomlinson restrained him.

The local paper came and I posed in front of our blackened front door. The photo was on the front page! My hair looked so cool.

Kiritimati

by Dougal Wilson-Croome

I will go back to Kiritimati one day. I have a globe on my desk and it's positioned so I can see it, always. I like to be reminded of 17th June 2002 when my life raft washed up on the shore of that tiny speck in the Pacific. I don't tell people Kiritimati is a large atoll, 124 square miles, when they ask about my survival. They can't grasp how small that is; how lucky I was. Look at a globe one day and imagine me, alone in a life raft in the Pacific.

Last Hotel

by Peter Winder

She patrolled the twilight corridors, past the coughing, rambling and sometimes sobbing of her 'guests'.

A sudden laugh alarmed her.

At the hotel laughs had been good; guests enjoying themselves. Incoherence coming from alcohol.

The red flash summoned her, like room service, to help with pain and panic, not for champagne and canapés. There were approaches and procedures, even for dying. At the hotel dying had been a disaster. No procedures. Shameful. Whispered.

She had shaken the pale, young woman and shouted, not accepting death.

Extended leave and sedatives failed her. She silently patrolled the twilight corridors.

Author Biographies

Sue Anderson

Sue Anderson lives on the borders of lots of things, including Wales. She loves science fiction and fantasy, and won the British Fantasy Society short story award in 2006. She's unhealthily obsessed by the idea of getting a novel into print.

Sarah Armstrong

Sarah Armstrong lives in Colchester with her husband, four children, four cats and four chickens. She is an Associate Lecturer with the Open University where she teaches Creative Writing. She has written a number of short stories and recently won a competition, Roman Voices, with 'Medusa'. One of her poems has also been selected to be displayed on the Polesworth Poetry Trail. When she is not writing, Sarah knits clothes (which she has been known to make her children wear) and crochets toys on demand for her nieces.

Holly Atkinson

Holly Atkinson completed her MA in Creative Writing at Bath Spa University in 2001 and has been writing in optimistic bursts ever since. One day she hopes a burst will be long and optimistic enough for her to complete her next novel. She grew up in the Peak District surrounded by crags and sheep, and now lives in Bristol and works as an administrator and a holistic massage therapist.

Christine Axon

After dreams of travelling the world, Christine got as far as France where she lived the Gaelic life for fourteen years. On her return to England, she gravitated toward a creative writing class that reformed as a multi-talented Writing Group several years ago. Now based in Lytham St Annes, Christine enjoys yoga, painting and the most escapist of art forms – storytelling.

K.M. Bainbridge

K.M. Bainbridge grew up in South Shields and read Philosophy and English Literature at Edinburgh; while there she divided her time between student journalism and singing with her band Bliss Point, whose finest hour was opening for Lindisfarne in 1972. *Sic transit gloria mundi.* After teaching English on Tyneside and in Durham for many years, she retrained as a Gestalt therapist and now lives in rural Northumberland, writing, reading, making music and watching animals.

Chloe Banks

Chloe Banks is a twenty-two year-old Christian who lives with her husband in Bristol. She has only just started writing regularly but would do nothing else if she had the choice. In 2006 an old school friend set her the challenge of writing a novel and the result, *No More Chocolate,* was short-listed for a undergraduate novel-writing award. She graduated in 2008 with a first-class science degree and is a qualified personal trainer.

Adam Bealby

Adam Bealby's first published work was a wee feature in computer game magazine *Zero* at the tender age of thirteen. Since then he's shot up a bit. He now lives in Worcestershire with his wife and two children and is currently writing lots of short stories. His work has more recently been published in indie comic book anthology *Fusion* and the award-winning *Red Eye Magazine*. When not making up stories he's still playing the same computer games he did in 1992.

Angus Binnie

Angus is a retired social worker and a long-time member of Tyne and Esk Writers' Group supported by Mid and East Lothian Libraries. He has had successes in their Annual Writing Competitions. Two of his short stories appeared in Scribble magazine and one in an anthology by Scottish Book Trust called *Days Like This*. Latterly his main output has been poetry with poems appearing in *East Lothian Life*. He published his wartime reminiscences under the title *A Teenage Soldier* (Calder Wood Press, Dunbar).

Jackie Blake

Jackie Blake lives in Lytham St Annes with her husband and teenage daughter. She is a founder member of the Fylde Brighter Writers writing circle and through this group has discovered a love of writing. She has had a couple of small successes on the publishing front but somehow finds that this has become less important than enjoying her writing and maintaining the circle of friends she has made through a shared love of writing.

John Blunden

John Blunden has been a cook, museum tour guide, and stand-up comedian. He has now decided that he would prefer to be a writer, and is currently studying Creative and Professional Writing at the University of Glamorgan.

Tom Bowen

Tom Bowen and his co-author, Noggin, live on a farm in Pembrokeshire. They are both in their seventies. In 1998, Noggin was acquired from Ty-Argored Animal Sanctuary. As a cross Corgi, Collie, Alsatian, he is an invaluable farm dog, although sometimes inclined to drive sheep back into the field out of which they had just been herded, a tendency perhaps attributable to his genetic mixture. Tom retired from a career in the Law, which he recalls as dazzling, whereas it was, in fact, indifferent. He thinks he has Noggin's complete loyalty and devotion. Apparently, he has got that wrong, too.

Sarah Boyd

Sarah Boyd was born in Scotland and lives in Perthshire. In 2005 she graduated from St Andrews University with a first-class degree in English and promptly returned there to complete an MLitt in Shakespeare Studies. After that she decided she didn't want to write about other people's books any more and set about writing her own stories for the first time since high school. Currently she's studying creative writing with the Open University and trying to fit her nocturnal writing habits into everyday life. The Nano-Fiction competition is the first writing competition she has entered and to her surprise and delight will also provide her first experience of being published.

Ruth Brandt

Ruth Brandt hasn't stopped writing since she accidentally enrolled in a creative writing evening class nine years ago. Her children and friends waste the time she puts aside to write, providing in return a pitiful amount of inspiration. One of her 2009 writing resolutions, to enter a competition a month, has been achieved so far, and she doggedly continues to face rejection by women's magazines by sending out further stories, although she has seen some success here. A completed novel gathers dust and another is gestating while she has a go at writing radio plays.

Rosie Brown

Rosie Brown lives on the beautiful North Norfolk coast and loves walking in the countryside at one with Nature, which is the main inspiration for her work. She has a degree in Fine Art. More recently she has found great encouragement from taking a ten-week UEA accredited course on poetry and in winning and being shortlisted for several writing competitions and published in magazines including *Countryside Tales* and *Earth Love,* which raises money for the environment. She often exhibits works that combine paint with words in which she tries, in an unsettled world, to invoke a sense of peace.

Lyn Browne

Lyn Browne lives on the edge of Dartmoor, and is a member of Moor Poets and Two Rivers Poets. Writing poetry helps her to be concise, and possibly opaque, when she tackles short stories. She was commended, and published, in Leaf Books microfiction competition last year, and though she has won prizes and been published, this is a rare first prize. Lyn went to university at forty, gaining an MA at Exeter five years later. She is married, has three children and two grandchildren spread over different continents. Luckily she enjoys travelling.

Linda Cairns

Linda organises running races – although she has had boring, sensible jobs in the past. She has a PhD in Food Science and has taught English and IT. Now Linda teaches orienteering and wants children to discover the fun of sport. Her husband coaches boys' football and their boys are into golf, football, orienteering and climbing. They live in Guildford. Linda tries to keep fit and aims to be green. She joined Anna McKerrow's class last year to realise her ambition and now it's a treat to curl up on a Sunday afternoon, after an exhausting run, with a laptop and write.

Jan Cascarini

During the sixties and seventies, Jan Cascarini worked in the theatre. She did stage management and lighting before marriage and children put a stop to it. In the mid-nineties she took up writing and has been indulging this interest, in a somewhat haphazard fashion, ever since. She writes short stories and occasionally plays, and hopes to produce at least one truly inspired piece before the old man with the scythe gets her.

Apala Chowdhury

Apala Chowdhury is a writer, waitress and tutor of children with dyslexia. She has been a newspaper journalist and a private detective. After the school run and her own (almost) daily (almost) three-mile run, Apala goes back to bed where she is writing her first novel. She lives with her two children in north London.

Mary Cookson

Mary Cookson was born in Birmingham but is now resident in the North West of England. In 1997 she did an undergraduate course at Edge Hill University and then an MA in Writing Studies. Medieval history is an all-consuming passion for Mary – at the drop of a hat she will compare the advantages of phlebotomy over leeches as a prevention and cure for illness to the medieval mind. She has completed a novel set in the fifteenth century. Her second novel, set in the 1970s, is at the stage where she is itching to return to the middle ages. She has had poetry, short pieces and stories published in small press magazines, newspapers and *Mslexia*.

Una Corbett

Una Corbett lives in Bristol. She has been an actor, a primary school teacher and now works with people addicted to tranquillisers. She has directed two award-winning productions for World Mental Health Day, performed and partly written by users of mental health services, as a result of which she is now a Mind Millennium Fellow. Una started writing six years ago on a whim. She is an enthusiastic member of a writing group in Bath, which inspires and keeps her going.

Dan Coxon

Dan Coxon is a freelance journalist and writer, and the author of the *Wee Book Of Scotland*. Having spent several years writing about the Scottish music scene for publications as diverse as *Is This Music?*, *Rock'n'Reel*, *Disorder* and *Artrocker*, he has recently relocated to the Pacific Northwest. He is currently editing both a novel manuscript and a non-fiction travelogue about New Zealand, while also maintaining a regular movie review blog at www.theflickerproject.com. His fiction has appeared in *Roadworks, The Third Alternative*, and in the 2008 anthology *Late-Night River Lights*.

Bobbie Darbyshire

Bobbie Darbyshire lives in Clapham. She won the 2008 fiction prize at the National Academy of Writing (president Melvyn Bragg), and has been published in their anthology, *Finding a Voice*, and in *Mslexia*. Her 1970s comedy of manners, *Truth Games*, comes out in July 2009 (www.cinnamonpress.com), and her mystery rom-com, *The Real McCoy*, has been serialised in a print magazine, *First Edition* (www.firsteditionpublishing. co.uk). Bobbie has worked as barmaid, mushroom picker, film extra, maths coach, cabinet minister's private secretary and care assistant, as well as in social research and policy. She runs a writers' group and is a volunteer adult-literacy teacher.

Shelley Day Sclater

Shelley Day Sclater was a lawyer and then an academic social scientist. Despite advice not to give up the day job, in 2005 she jumped off the treadmill and now earns a crust freelancing. An Open University short course in 2006 rekindled a long-standing passion for fiction, and she now has a ton of work-in-progress: a novel, loads of short stories, and a sort of fictionalised memoir. She's seriously thinking of doing the MA in Creative Writing at Newcastle. Shelley lives in a tiny cottage on the Northumberland coast.

Morgan Downie

Morgan Downie is one of the many and varied islands of the mythic archipelago of Scotia. Its people believe in the guiding power of cats, love unconditional, the blue smartie, the clean beauty of a perfect breaking wave and the notion that at least one in six statements should be untrue.

Nicholas Edwards

Nicholas Edwards, twenty-seven, was born, raised and still lives in London. He recently took up writing after taking an introductory day at CityLit. As well as trying his hand at a variety of writing styles in his spare time he dabbles in song writing and practices yoga.

Anne Elder

Anne Elder grew up in the North of England and studied Russian at Leeds University. She works part-time as an assistant to a surveyor and writes in her spare time, particularly short stories about possible future scenarios. She has won several prizes in national writing competitions as well as having been published in a well-known women's magazine. She lives in Leeds with her husband, two children and three cats.

Gavin Eyers

Gavin Eyers is mid-way through a degree in Literature, has just completed a first draft of his first novel and is slowly working on a collection of short stories. He works in a post room in the mornings, gyms and swims in the afternoons, writes and studies after that then often settles for the evening in one of the wonderful old pubs of Greenwich, South-East London, the town in which he lives and which he loves. Gavin has previously been published in the Leaf Books anthology, *Discovering a Comet and More Micro-Fiction*.

Amelia Fortnam

Amelia Fortnam is eighteen and is a student in her lower sixth year at Sixth Form College in Cambridge. She is taking her AS-Level English Literature exam this spring, and looks forward greatly to her inevitable failure. Failure, as we all know, brings a kind of freedom for the fail-ee. She has been writing stories, short and long, since she was seven. Her Leaf Nano-Fiction competition entry was a landmark for her: the first time she sent a piece of work to a publisher.

Wayne Foster

Wayne Foster has been a pizza chef, a burger flipper, a landscape gardener, a bouncer, a dishwasher, a transport inspector, and today he calls himself an academic. He has previously worked as a ghost-writer and continues to write short stories with varying success. He is always threatening to finish a novel. Wayne's critical interests include the work of Don DeLillo and David Foster Wallace. He believes that *Infinite Jest* is the great contemporary novel.

Dorothy Fryd

Dorothy Fryd is a writer and performance poet, who has presented her work at various venues in London, including the Roundhouse, the Poetry Café (Poetry Podcast Launch) and Brixtongue Art Gallery. She is working on a short story collection and a play. She teaches poetry and creative writing workshops in primary/secondary schools and is currently working on the 2009 Lynk Reach London Teenage Poetry Slam Project. Dorothy also studies at South Bank in London and lives in Kent with her two children, Eva and Jack.

Clare Girvan

Clare escaped from inner-city teaching in Birmingham in 1995 to live in Devon with her journalist husband and three cats, and pursue her long-awaited writing career. She has temporarily shelved, but not abandoned, a novel in favour of writing plays, which vary in length from one minute to two hours. Many have won prizes and been performed, particularly in Cambridge, where her one-acters seem to do quite well. Remaining ambitions: to have a play performed in a London theatre, publish the/a novel and win the Bridport short story competition. And the Booker would be nice.
See website: www.claregirvan.co.uk

Dee Gordon

Dee sold scores of romantic picture scripts in the sixties and seventies to such iconic magazines as *Valentine, Romeo, Mirabelle*, and *Marilyn*, returning to writing after selling her recruitment business in 2000. She can now boast a published novel (*Meat Market*, set in the recruitment industry), a poetry anthology (*Bad Girls*), and five non-fiction books on local history (Southend and Essex). Another Essex book is due out at the end of 2009 and she is working on two commissions currently, another about Southend, and one about Stepney, East London, where she has her roots. She lives in Westcliff-on-Sea with her husband and autistic son, and gives talks about her writing and her books to raise money for Southend Mencap. More info on www.AuthorsRegister.com/deegordon.

Ellie Hartland

Ellie Hartland is thirty-five and lives in the North-East Essex countryside. She has been writing short fiction and novels since the age of nine. Her work is both dark and disturbing and she likes nothing more than creating characters that bury themselves deep in the readers' psyche and return to haunt them in the dead of night. Ellie is 'owned' by two psychotic cats and is currently studying BA (Hons) Writing at Anglia Ruskin University in Cambridge. It is her ambition to one day be able to live on the proceeds of writing novels full time.

Sarah Hilary

Sarah is an award-winning writer whose fiction appears in *Smokelong Quarterly*, *The Fish Anthology 2008*, *Prick of the Spindle*, *The Best of Every Day Fiction*, and in the Crime Writers' Association anthology, *MO: Crimes of Practice*. A column about the wartime experiences of her mother, who was a child internee of the Japanese, was published in the Spring 09 edition of *Foto8 Magazine*.
www.sarah-crawl-space.blogspot.com.

Michelle Holhorea

Michelle lives in Bedfordshire; she has, oddly enough, a degree in mining engineering, earns her living as an office administrator and, in her spare time, likes to bring out her creative side. She enjoys meddling with brushes and colours in what she calls her amateur painting, and experimenting with ideas, herbs and spices in the kitchen, but most of all she loves writing. Michelle rediscovered the joy of toying with words three years ago when she joined the online writing community Great Writing. Her dearest wish is to see the novel she's currently working on, her first, in print.

Linda Houlton

Linda Houlton is a writer based on Merseyside. Her work has been included in a wide range of magazines and anthologies including *Listening to the Birth of Crystals* and *Extra Extra*. Linda has performed her work on television and radio and has given readings at events around Liverpool including Face of the City (2008) and Climate for Change (2009). A member of the University of Liverpool Creative Writing Society, Linda has been the judge of the International Ted Walters Short Story and Poetry Competition for the last three years.

Lauren Huxley-Blythe

Lauren lives in Lancashire near to the sea and also in Dublin close to Sandymount Strand. A passion for literature has inspired her studies, teaching and writing. She is currently working on a novella, *Dandelions*. She adores her wonderful, beautiful family especially when they get to hang out together and eat cake. If there is cricket is on the radio that's even better.

Flavia Idriceanu

Flavia Idriceanu is a Romanian conference interpreter and devoted day-dreamer. She writes in English because she thinks that the only way to deal with prepositions in a foreign language is to be creative about them. She lives in Bucharest and until now she has only shared her short stories with a handful of friends. She is co-author of *Legends of Blood. The Vampire in History and Myth* (Sutton Publishing, 2005). Written together with historian W.B. Bartlett, this book is an attempt to follow the structure of the vampire myth and its development throughout history.

Kathy Kachelries

Kathy Kachelries grew up in a suburb of Philadelphia, Pennsylvania, but her wanderlust has forced her into the life of a nomadic English teacher. She's taken a break from her travels to pursue an MFA in Critical Studies, and she currently resides in California. Two years ago, she created the daily flash fiction site www.365tomorrows.com, and she remains an editor and occasional contributor. Her material needs are few: Kathy has been known to survive for weeks on nothing but coffee and a blank notebook.

Grace Knight

Grace Knight is twenty-five and lives with her mates in East London. She writes plays and has just worked up the courage to start sending them to people. She has a first class degree in English Literature and Philosophy from Cardiff University, which is where she first started writing micro-fiction. Grace is pathologically sociable, and spends a lot of time trying to coerce people into keeping her company while she writes.

R.J. Marer

R.J. lives in the Lake District, England, and engages in writing with greater frequency than bathing. Possessed by a lustful appetite for literature, there is the hope of a lifelong affair between writer, words and audience.

Pauline Masurel

Pauline Masurel lives in the South West of England and is an allotment gardener who is about to lose her plot. She enjoys writing tiny stories, non-linear fiction and mini-autobiographies. Her micro-fiction, 'Discovering a Comet', was published in the eponymous Leaf collection. She performs with the Bristol-based Heads & Tales group. Her work has variously been featured in print, online and broadcast on radio. She was shortlisted for the 2008 Asham Award. Details of her writing and collaborations can be found at her website www.unfurling.net.

Emily Midorikawa

Emily Midorikawa, twenty-nine, was brought up in Yorkshire and has moved around a lot. At the moment she lives in Worcestershire, where she works in a library in a small market town. Emily holds an MA in Creative Writing from UEA. Her work has been published in various magazines and anthologies, including *Aesthetica, Dream Catcher* and *Mslexia*. An early riser, she writes before work each morning and believes in carrying a pen and paper at all times. She is close to completing her first novel, a story about loss set in Ōsaka, Japan.

Beverley Mulliner

Beverley works for the NHS in Cornwall and is also a Reiki healer. She has written for as long as she can remember but, despite numerous attempts, has never been published before. The acceptance of a piece by Leaf Books has spurred her on to further endeavours. Despite enjoying her 'day job', working from home is her main objective and she sees both writing and Reiki as fulfilling ways to achieve this.

Lyn O'Kelly

Lyn O'Kelly is a full-time English and Writing student at Anglia Ruskin University, Cambridge. She has been writing for four years since the age of fifteen, and this is her first published short story. Besides writing, her main passion in life is music and she looks forward to moving to New York to finish her degree and start a career in music journalism. For her ability to persist and succeed in writing, she thanks her favourite author, Margaret Atwood, her favourite bands and their inspirational words, and her best friend – for giving her the encouragement and push she needed.

Phil O'Shea

Phil O'Shea is a writer and stand-up comedian living in Edinburgh. He has just completed a Masters in Screenwriting at Screen Academy Scotland, and has written and performed several plays and sketches in various venues throughout Scotland. This year, he is continuing to perform stand-up comedy and is bringing his new play *Underwater Cathedral* to the fringe festival in August.

Gavin Parish

Gavin has previously had some of his nano-fiction published in the Wonderful World of Worders anthology (2007). In 2008 he entered Soho Theatre's Westminster Prize with a 10-minute play that wasn't ranked – in 2009 he made it through to the second round. Next year he's aiming to be an 'also-ran' or maybe even a runner-up. In the meantime he's working in turns on a novel, a film script and several smaller teleplays, and actually finishing stuff! He reckons nano-fiction clamps down on verbosity, sharpens the mind, and helps with all that vital business of beginnings, middles and … (transmission ends).

Jonathan Pinnock

Jonathan Pinnock was born in Bedfordshire, and – despite having so far visited over forty other countries – has failed to relocate any further away than the next-door and equally unexceptional county of Hertfordshire. He is married with two children, several cats and a 1961 Ami Continental jukebox. His work has won several prizes, shortlistings and longlistings, and he has been published in such diverse publications as Smokebox, Every Day Fiction and Necrotic Tissue. His unimaginatively-titled yet moderately interesting website may be found at www.jonathanpinnock.com.

Pamela Pottinger

Pamela Pottinger lives and works in rural Cumbria. The mother of three home-educated children, she has in the past spent much of her time driving them about and subsequently waiting for them ... car parks and side streets in winter are not a lot of fun unless you have something to occupy youself with, hence the fact that at least 50% of her writing is done on the back seat of her car. She writes mainly short stories and poetry, some of which have found homes in various anthologies, some broadcast on radio. She has also recently made a foray into performing her own work with Spotlight, an arts funded initiative that operates in Lancaster.

John Ravenscroft

John has loads of short stories hiding away in the computer. He attends workshops given by Sue Johnson in Pershore. Newly retired, he decided to follow his dream and write. Nothing published until now. For that he thanks Leaf Books. John is struggling to write a novel but is now wondering if it is the right subject as he is running out of steam. Still, the enjoyment of writing is the main attraction and he is in no rush to finish it. Nano-fiction provides the ultimate in editing skills.

Clare Reddaway

Clare Reddaway escaped television drama to indulge in an MA in Creative Writing at Bath Spa University. She now writes scripts, short stories, articles and reviews. She can be spotted performing around the south-west as a member of live fiction group Heads and Tales. Her radio play *Laying Ghosts* was recently recorded by the Wireless Theatre Company. Two of her stories for children will be published by Bridge House later this year. A number of her (very short) stage plays have been performed by WriteOn in Cambridge. She lives in Bath with her daughter, a dog and two cats.

Jemma Regan

Jemma Regan, aged twenty-six and from Manchester, started writing mythical tales aged six and has written a diary every night for the last twenty years. They are hidden in a box under her bed. She has spent the last three years travelling around the world, mostly in South America, Australia and Canada. Cuba and India made the most formidable impressions on her and she is currently attempting to get her first novel – set in India – published. She has a first class honours degree in Philosophy and Theology from Durham University. This is the first writing competition she has entered.

Martin Richards

Martin Richards works as an architectural draughtsman. He has recently started to pursue his interest in writing fiction, seeing it as a natural progression from his days as a songwriter. He has a wife, Sally and two children, Isla and Thomas. They live near the former mining town of Camborne in West Cornwall.

Andy Rigley

Andy lives in Derby with his wife, three kids, Seth the cat and Avril the rat. Andy has always written and once had a story published in the *Derby Evening Telegraph*. He is currently studying part time, for a Certificate in Creative Writing at Nottingham University. This is the first time he's submitted work to a competition in over eight years. When not writing, Andy can be found (or not) alone in the hills around Derbyshire, finding abandoned castles, canals and railways in the local area, or messing about on the river in his boat. He has a lemon tree.

Gary Robins

Gary Robins lives in Newport and is interested in contemporary culture, social history and popular music. He gained a degree and postgraduate diploma (English) at the University of Wales, Newport, as a mature student, where he took up writing and photography. He has had a non fiction book, *Prefabrications*, published by Ffotogallery/University of Wales, written a short play, *Bitter Harvest*, which was publicly read by Made In Wales Theatre Company, written an article on nostalgia for the next issue of *The Raconteur Magazine*, and is an accomplished songwriter. Gary is currently working on a collection of short stories.

Nancy Saunders

Nancy Saunders lives in a Hampshire village and works in Library Acquisitions, unpacking lovely new books and sending them out to hungry readers. Writing, fiddle-playing and enjoying the great outdoors are all squeezed in around the job. Her writing has won a couple of prizes and appeared here and there online and in small literary magazines. Elly and Oscar are Nancy's two true significant others.

Jackie Sullivan

Jackie Sullivan is a writer / artist who has worked as Head of Visual and Performing Arts in a London College, lectured widely in visual art and creative writing and worked as a professional artist. She currently spends her time between London and Chicago where she is pursuing both painting and writing, specifically micro-fiction, which is emerging as her preferred form. Non-fiction pieces have appeared in the Telegraph and London area magazines and her micro-fiction regularly appears in the literary magazine Tears in the Fence and micro-fiction anthologies.

Jayne Thickett

Jayne Thickett is thirty-six years old. She has been previously published in 5photostory.com's 2007/08 anthology and once did a translation of Beowulf, but she was eleven years old and might have been out on a couple of things. She has various short stories out in the wilderness and a novel constantly berating her for her procrastination.

Andrew Thorn

Andrew Thorn is currently seeking an agent to represent his recently completed novel for young people, The Downside of Dying, about a teenage accident-victim's attempts to escape from the afterlife. Andrew, together with his wife Jarek, runs Timezones Curriculum Support Ltd. For twenty years they have written and produced educational shows and workshops for schools and heritage sites: visit their website www.timezones. demon.co.uk for more information about their work.

Sandy Tippett

Sandy Tippett is a published author, editor and translator. She prefers writing short stories, nano fiction and twiction (on her twitter account as greensandy). She is a polyglot interested in the environment, family and community - all of which feature in her writing. As well as writing and lecturing she organises greener writing events which can be found at www.greenergetaways. org. Join her in August 2009 for the next 'Write in Edinburgh' event!

Robin Tompkins

Robin is from Birmingham, where he has been telling stories all his life like his father before him and writing them down for nearly as long. He has also been known to paint a bit and take photographs that some people quite like. He enjoys many things, including and especially cats, beer and Theremins. Robin is also quite fond of being published but has only managed it twice so far. With the exception of Cats and being published, all his other enthusiasms are subject to change without notice.

Steve Tymms

Steve lives in Hertfordshire with his wife, and they have four children. He works as a software developer for an investment bank (this is correct at the time of writing!). Steve and his wife went on a creative writing taster course, and that was where he got bitten by the writing bug. As well as short stories, he would like to be able to write radio comedy. Steve and some of his children do DJ-ing and party organising. Steve has also been known to sing, act and dance, sometimes even all together.

Wendy Vaughan

Wendy Vaughan has roamed from the Isle of Ely via work in the theatre and teaching children with special educational needs to the Isle of Thanet where she lives in contended retirement. From her beach hut she enjoys the Turneresque sunsets while trying to organise random words into short stories that are now and again put into print. She dreams of one day writing something longer. When frustrated she occasionally stamps her feet in a Flamenco class.

Pete Walsh

Pete Walsh lives aboard a narrowboat in Nottinghamshire where he dabbles in art and photography, and writes inspired mainly by the natural environment. Although he has a novel in the making, he writes poetry and short stories. Several of his poems are published in online magazines, since becoming a part-time student of Creative Writing at the University of Nottingham, and he is very pleased to see his work in the anthology.

Guy Ware

Guy Ware is a recovering Civil Servant. He has published stories in competition collections and anthologies from Comma Press, Route, Apis Books, Leaf Press and others, and on the internet at www.decongested.com. In *Time Out* Nicholas Royle described Guy's *Witness Protection* as 'a remarkably successful story – the best I have read for a long, long time'.

Robert Warrington

Robert Warrington lives at the bottom of a warm, shallow sea. Or he would have done in the Silurian Period. Fortunately for him (as he hates total immersion), the sea has been replaced by land and is currently known as the Black Country, where he is a playwright, poet etc.

Sue Wilsea

Sue Wilsea lives in a village near Hull on the banks of The Humber. In an earlier life she had short stories published but took a twenty-five year break to cultivate a teaching career and four children. Now semi-retired and with her offspring having (more or less) left home she should have No Excuses to avoid writing. However, she continues to find diversions ranging from being a luvvie with the local Dramatic Society to walking, cooking and reading trashy magazines. This flippancy is an attempt to mask the fact that she is – and always has been, it seems – working on a novel.

Dougal Wilson-Croome

Back in the Wye Valley after a period flying aeroplanes into the world's hot spots – Luanda, Kabul, Baghdad, Khartoum – and determined not to return to a past life as a Chartered Accountant to make ends meet, Dougal spends his time walking the hills looking at geology as part of his studies in geoscience and training for his next marathon. He has always had a love affair with the written word and currently writes short stories, with a passion for flash fiction.

Peter Winder

Peter Winder has been writing for pleasure for a long time. In recent years he has concentrated on short stories, which he collects into small booklets and distributes to friends. He is also in the process of writing a crime novel.